Yellow Umbrella Books are published by Capstone Press
151 Good Counsel Drive, P.O. Box 669, Mankato, Minnesota 56002
http://www.capstone-press.com

Copyright © 2001 Capstone Press. All rights reserved.
No part of this book may be reproduced without written permission
from the publisher. The publisher takes no responsibility for the use of any
of the materials or methods described in this book, nor for the products thereof.
Printed in the United States of America.

Library of Congress Cataloging-in-Publication Data
Trumbauer, Lisa, 1963–
   Teamwork/by Lisa Trumbauer.
   p. cm.
   Includes index.
   ISBN 0-7368-0733-0
   1.Team learning approach in education—Juvenile literature. 2. Cooperativeness—Juvenile
literature. [1. Cooperativeness.] I. Title.
LB1032.T77   2001
302.3′4—dc21   00-038219

Summary: Describes teamwork, including working together, playing together, and
studying together.

Editorial Credits:
Susan Evento, Managing Editor/Product Development; Elizabeth Jaffe, Senior Editor;
   Charles Hunt, Designer; Kimberly Danger and Heidi Schoof, Photo Researchers

Photo Credits:
Cover: Visuals Unlimited/Mark Gibson; Title Page: Unicorn Stock Photos/Aneal Vohra; Page
2: Pictor; Page 3: International Stock/Nicole Katano; Page 4: Index Stock Imagery; Page 5:
Index Stock Imagery; Page 6: Index Stock Imagery; Page 7: Shaffer Photography/James L.
Shaffer (top & bottom); Page 8: Visuals Unlimited/Mark Gibson; Page 9: Unicorn Stock
Photos/Steve Bourgeois (top), Jane Faircloth/Transparencies, Inc. (bottom); Page 10: Index
Stock Imagery; Page 11: Index Stock Imagery; Page 12: Photo Network/Amy Lundstrom; Page
13: Shaffer Photography/James L. Shaffer; Page 14: Unicorn Stock Photos/Dennis MacDonald
(top), Index Stock Imagery (bottom); Page 15: Index Stock Imagery (top), Unicorn Stock
Photos/Shellie Nelson (bottom); Page 16: Photo Network/Tom McCarthy

1 2 3 4 5 6 06 05 04 03 02 01

Teamwork

By Lisa Trumbauer

Consulting Editor: Gail Saunders-Smith, Ph.D.
Consultants: Claudine Jellison and Patricia Williams,
Reading Recovery Teachers
Content Consultant: Tammy Huber, Youth Education Director,
North Dakota Farmers Union

Yellow Umbrella Books

an imprint of Capstone Press
Mankato, Minnesota

I like to play alone.

I like to play with others too.

I like to work alone.

I like to work with others too.

Many things are easier to do
when you have help.
People helping one another
to get something done
is called teamwork.

Children
in this class
have jobs.

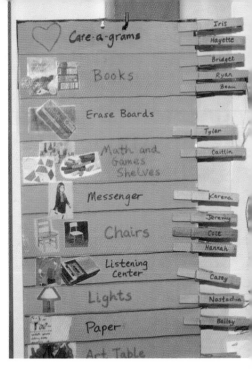

These children
work together
to clean
their classroom.

7

A baseball team needs
many players. Each player
has a part to play.

Together, the
teammates play
another team.
Go teamwork!

Sometimes learning
with a team is fun.
You can ask
each other questions.

Together, you can find answers.
This is teamwork.

Sometimes you learn
how to do things alone.

Then you can use
what you learned
to work or play with others.

Teammates like
to work and play
together.

It feels good
to be part
of a team.

This is teamwork.

Garbage

Glass

Paper

When are you part of a team?

Words to Know/Index

Word Count: 148
Early-Intervention Levels: 9–12